MONSTER SHOES

Emma Laybourn
Illustrated by Georgien Overwater

To Sarah and Peter

Series reading consultant: Prue Goodwin,
Reading and Language Information Centre,
University of Reading

A CORGI PUPS BOOK : 0 552 54634 8

First publication in Great Britain

PRINTING HISTORY
Corgi Pups edition published 1999

3 5 7 9 10 8 6 4 2

Set in Bembo Schoolbook by
Phoenix Typesetting, Ilkley, West Yorkshire.

Corgi Books are published by Transworld Publishers,
61-63 Uxbridge Road, London W5 5SA,
a division of The Random House Group Ltd,
in Australia by Random House Australia (Pty) Ltd,
20 Alfred Street, Milsons Point, Sydney, NSW 2061, Australia,
in New Zealand by Random House New Zealand Ltd,
18 Poland Road, Glenfield, Auckland 10, New Zealand
and in South Africa by Random House (Pty) Ltd,
Endulini, 5a Jubilee Road, Parktown 2193, South Africa.

The Random House Group Limited supports The Forest Stewardship
Council® (FSC®), the leading international forest-certification organisation.
Our books carrying the FSC label are printed on FSC®-certified paper.
FSC is the only forest-certification scheme supported by the leading
environmental organisations, including Greenpeace. Our
paper procurement policy can be found at
www.randomhouse.co.uk/environment

MIX
Paper from
responsible sources
FSC® C016897

Printed and bound in Great Britain by Clays Ltd, St Ives PLC

Contents

Chapter One

I was fed up.

I'd spent all morning trying
on shoes. Big, black, shiny shoes.
Some were too loose. Some were
too tight. And they were all too
expensive.

"Let's go home!" I begged.
"We've been in every single shoe
shop!"

"You need new shoes for
school, Jack," said Mum.

"I hate new shoes! Why can't
I wear my trainers?"

"Because they're scruffy and squishy. They're falling to bits."

"I like them scruffy and squishy!" I said. "It took me ages to get them that way!"
Mum sighed.

"Maybe we'd better go," she said.

She turned – and stopped dead.

"Look! Why didn't I see that shop before?"

Right behind us a big sign said:

MONSTER SHOE SALE

"It wasn't there before!" I said.
I didn't like the look of that
shop. It was as dark and narrow
as a cave.

But Mum dived in. I had to
follow her.

Inside, shoes were piled every-where. You never saw such shoes!

Pink shoes, yellow shoes, stripy shoes, shoes with buttons, and feathers, and bows . . .

"Yuck," I said. "They're all horrible! They're monster shoes!

10

I can't wear any of these to
school. Let's go!"

"*Aha!*" said Mum. She pointed
to the top of a pile.

A pair of gleaming, black
lace-ups sat there. Shoes lay
tumbled around them, as if
they'd been kicked aside . . .

11

They were the blackest,
shiniest shoes I'd ever seen. They
shone like polished stone.

I touched one. It felt like
stone, too – cold and hard.

"Just the thing," said Mum.
"And they're your size! Try them
on, Jack."

The shoes felt stiff and heavy.
I couldn't tie the laces properly.
Mum did them for me.

"Now walk around!" she said.
I clomped up and down. The
shoes creaked as I walked, with a
horrible creak, like a door
opening – a door into a dark,
spooky room . . .

"They're too noisy!" I said.

"That'll wear off," said Mum.

"They're too heavy!"

"Good! They might slow you down a bit."

"They're too big!"

"Plenty of room for growth,"
said Mum. "With luck, they
might last you all year."

All year! I couldn't wear these
monster shoes *all year*!

With shaking fingers I tore at
the laces.

"I can't get them off!" I
wailed.

"You can wear them home,"
said Mum. She walked towards
the till. I stomped after her like
an elephant.

"Mum! Wait!"

But Mum was already paying. I was trapped inside a pair of Monster Shoes!

Chapter Two

"Get up, Jack!" said Mrs Pickett.
"What's wrong with you
today?"

I scrambled to my feet.
"Nothing, Mrs Pickett!"

But I knew what was wrong.
It was the Monster Shoes.

It was the first day I'd worn
them to school. I'd tied the laces
as tightly as I could.

But those laces just wouldn't
stay tied. They were as slippery
as snakes. They kept on untying
themselves when I wasn't
looking, and tripping me up.

Crash! I fell over the computer.

Smash! I stumbled into the sink.

Whoosh! I slid under the maths table.

Mrs Pickett got really cross.

"For goodness' sake, Jack!" she said. "Do up your shoelaces *properly*!"

I felt myself turn red. She thought I couldn't tie my shoelaces!

"I *have*!" I protested. "They just won't stay done up. Look!"

I lifted my foot up to show her. Well, I sort of kicked it up. I was just as surprised as she was when a Monster Shoe flew off my foot and sailed through the air.

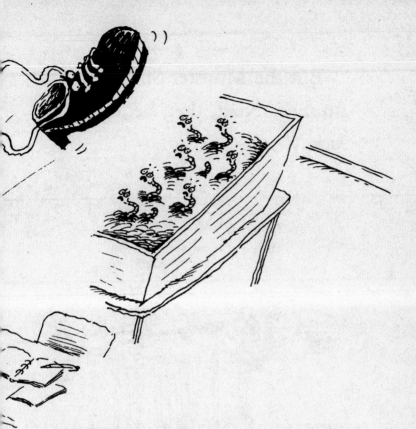

It landed in the wormery. Soil went everywhere.

After I said, "Sorry," to Mrs Pickett and the worms, I had to sweep it all up. It took me ages.

But the Monster Shoes hadn't finished. Next, they began to *kick*.

They kicked chairs. They kicked table legs. They kicked people's feet. I didn't make them kick – they just did it.

"Ouch!" said Katie. "That's
my ankle!"

"Oi!" said Asif. "That's my
chair!"

"Jack!" said Mrs Pickett.
"That's enough!"

I had to go and sit quietly in
the reading corner.

The shoes dug into me. I took
them off and glared at them. I
was furious!

A pair of scissors lay on the
bookcase. They gave me an idea.
I glanced around: nobody was
watching. If I cut up the laces, I
couldn't wear those shoes any
more . . .

But the laces wouldn't cut.
They were as tough as wire!

I jabbed at the leather. The scissors didn't even scratch it! My blood ran cold.

"I've got to get rid of these shoes!" I thought.

Quickly, I shoved them under the bookcase, as far as they

would go. Nobody could see
them there.

At playtime I lined up with
everyone else.

"Jack!" called Mrs Pickett.
"Put your shoes on."

"I can't find them, Miss!"

"Don't be silly," said Mrs Pickett crossly. "*There* they are!"

I stared. The Monster Shoes stood in the middle of the floor.

They'd escaped! They seemed to be grinning at me . . .

Those Monster Shoes were out to get me!

Chapter Three

I clumped home, longing for my lovely, scruffy trainers. I couldn't wait to put them on. Then I'd go and play football with my friend, Daniel . . .

But the Monster Shoes creaked at me, as if they were laughing. The sneaky, snaky laces kept on trying to trip me up. I tumbled through the front door, pulled off those horrible shoes and hurled them into the hall cupboard.

Bliss! My feet were free at last!

"Mum!" I yelled. "Where are my trainers?"

She yelled back, "In the hall cupboard, where they belong."

Quickly I threw open the cupboard door. And I *howled*. Mum came running.

"What is it? What's the matter?"

"My trainers!" I sobbed. I held them up.

One was split right through the sole. The other had a huge hole in its toe.

"The Monster Shoes ate my trainers!" I wailed. From deep inside the cupboard the Monster Shoes gleamed wickedly at me. They looked like two eyes in a dark cave.

"Rubbish!" said Mum briskly. "Your trainers are worn out,

that's all. They'll have to go in the bin. Lucky you've got your nice new shoes! Wear them instead."

"I can't!"

"Of course you can! Why not?"

How could I explain? Mum thought the Monster Shoes were wonderful. She didn't understand.

So in the end, I went to play football with Daniel wearing the Monster Shoes.

Daniel ran ahead. I couldn't run. I could only lumber. The

Monster Shoes creaked and groaned with every step. By the time we reached the park, I was groaning too.

Daniel tossed the ball to me. I took a kick at it – and then I *knew*.

The Monster Shoes didn't like football!

They wouldn't kick straight. They wouldn't dribble. All they would do was fall over the ball, and their laces, and each other.

"Sixteen—nil to me!" sang
Daniel happily.

I gritted my teeth. I was going
to score a goal, whether the
shoes liked it or not!

I drew back my left foot. I kicked with all my might.

BLAT! Through the air whizzed – not the football – but a *Monster Shoe*! It just missed an old man, walking his dog.

"Careful!" he shouted, as he threw it back.

Well, that did it! I was hopping mad with those Monster Shoes. I wasn't going to let them beat me!

Angrily I put the shoe back on. I laced up both shoes as tight as I could, with a double bow and a triple reef knot. When I'd

finished, the laces looked like
huge black lumps.

"You won't come off now!" I
said.

Then I kicked the ball again.

BLAM! This time the ball flew
straight and fast. So fast that it
shot past the goalposts! It hurtled

over the
bushes! It
landed with
a SPLAT in a
giant patch
of mud!

"What did you do that for?"
yelled Daniel. "That's my best
football!"

I ran to fetch it. But as soon as
I trod in the mud, it went
SQUELCH. I stopped.

"I want my ball back!"
complained Daniel.

"All right!" I said. "I'll get it."

I strode into
the mud. My
feet went
SQUELCH as
they went in,
and SLURP as
they came out.

Mud crept higher and higher around my shoes. Then I felt it ooze down inside them, cold and treacly.

At last I reached the football. I grabbed it and threw it to Daniel.

Then I tried to walk back.
I couldn't move.

The mud sucked at my
Monster Shoes. I couldn't pull
them out.

And I was sinking . . .

Chapter Four

"Take your shoes off!" shouted Daniel.

I tried. I yanked at the laces.

The double bows and triple reef
knots were slimy with mud. I
couldn't undo them.

I tried to pull my feet out of
the shoes. But they wouldn't
come off! They gripped my feet
like iron fists.

They wanted
to pull me
down into
the mud!

"Help!" I
cried. "I'll
drown!"

A deep voice spoke.

"Get hold of my stick!"

It was the old man I'd nearly
hit with my Monster Shoe. He
stood next to Daniel, holding
out his walking stick towards
me.

I stretched out for it. My fingers touched it, grabbed it, and held on tight.

The old man pulled at the stick. The shoes pulled at my feet. They wouldn't let go!

Then, slowly – ever so slowly – I felt one foot slide out of its shoe, like the cork out of a bottle. The other followed.

"Move quickly!" ordered the old man. "Or you'll get stuck again!"

I floundered through the mud.
A minute later, I was standing
on the path in filthy socks.

Behind me lay the Monster
Shoes, still sinking.

I felt like cheering. I'd never seen such a wonderful sight! The Monster Shoes were about to disappear for ever! Perhaps in a few thousand years scientists would dig them up, fossilized in the mud. "Ah! Tyrannoshoe-rus Rex," they'd say . . .

I grinned at the old man.

"Thanks," I said. "You've done me a really good turn!"

He looked pleased. "I'll try and do you another one!" he said.

He reached out again with his stick — this time with the hooked end. He leaned over and fished in the mud.

There was the loudest SLURP
I ever heard, like a giant with a
lollipop and no manners.

And out of the mud, black
and bedraggled, rose a Monster
Shoe.

"There!" said the old man proudly. He fished for the second shoe. "You'll have to clean them up. But at least your mum won't need to buy you new shoes!"

I looked at the slimy, dripping Monsters. Their gleam had gone. They were sticky and shapeless. I smiled weakly.

"Thanks a million," I said.

Chapter Five

The Monster Shoes looked
weird.

Mum had washed them under
the outside tap. She'd stuffed
them with newspaper until they
were dry. Then she'd attacked
them with shoe polish and a
brush. She'd thrown away the
laces, and put new ones in.

And they looked . . . weird.

"Oh, dear!" said Mum.

The Monster Shoes had lost
their wicked shine. They weren't
as hard and cold as stone any
more.

They were lumpy and bumpy
and dull and crinkly. They
looked like old, old shoes.

In fact – they looked pretty
good!

"They look dreadful!" said
Mum in despair. "I can't send
you to school in those! We'll
have to throw them away."

"No!" I clutched at the shoes.
"They look fine!"

I put them on.

"They feel fine!"

It was true — they did. They felt soft and squishy. The new laces were easy to tie.

I walked up and down. Not a creak.

 Mum
sighed, and
shook her
head.

"I suppose
they'll have
to do for now," she said. "I can't
afford to buy another pair just
yet."

"Don't worry!" I told her,
practising kicks. "They've got
plenty of room for growth. They
might even last all year!"

"All year!" said Mum,
horrified. "Oh, no! You can't
wear those all year!"

But I wasn't listening.

I was already running off in my squishy, scruffy, nice Tame Monster Shoes.

THE END